SATAN'S CIRCUS

BY

LADY ELEANOR SMITH

British Library Cataloguing-in-Publication Data
A catalogue record for this book is available from
the British Library

Contents

LADY ELEANOR SMITH

Lady Eleanor Furneaux Smith was born in Birkenhead, England in 1902. She had a privileged upbringing, and during her youth, her father – the well-known politician F. E. Smith – regaled her with macabre fairy tales, and encouraged her constantly to read. After her schooling, Smith worked as a society reporter and cinema critic for a number of London newspapers, before going on to travel with circuses as a publicist. A lifelong aficionado of gypsy culture (she possessed Romani heritage, stemming from her great-grandmother), Smith relished life with the circus, travelling widely on the continent and gaining much inspiration for her later novels. In the thirties, she turned to writing, and her first two novels, *Flamenco* (1931) and *Red Wagon* (1933) were instant bestsellers.

Much of her work, including a number of her short stories, provided the inspiration for a number of 'Gainsborough melodrama' films of the period. Her *The Man in Grey* (1943), adapted for the screen in the same year it was published, was a particular success.

Satan's Circus

by LADY ELEANOR SMITH

I ONCE asked a circus artist whom I knew to have worked at one time with the Circus Brandt whether or not he had enjoyed travelling with this well-known show. His reply was a curious one. Swiftly distorting his features into a hideous grimace, he spat violently upon the floor. Not another word would he say. My curiosity was, however, aroused, and I went next to an old Continental clown, now retired, who had the reputation of knowing every European circus as well as he knew his own pocket.

"The Circus Brandt," he said thoughtfully. "Well, you know, the Brandts are queer people, and have an odd reputation. They are Austrian, and their own country-people call them gipsies, by which they mean nomads, for the Brandts never pitch in their own land, but wander the whole world over as though the devil himself were at their heels. In fact, some call them 'Satan's Circus'."

"I thought," I said, "that the Circus Brandt was supposed to be a remarkably fine show?"

"It is," he said, and lit his pipe; "it's expensive, ambitious, showy, well run. In their way these people are artists, and

3

deserve more success than they have had. It's hard to say why they're so unpopular, but the fact remains that no one will stay with them more than a few months; and, what's more, wherever they go—India, Australia, Rumania, Spain, or Africa—they leave behind them a nasty, unpleasant sort of reputation as regards unpaid bills—which," he added, blowing smoke into the air, "is odd, for the Brandts are rich."

"How many Brandts are there?" I inquired, for I wished to know more about Europe's most elusive circus.

"You ask too many questions," said he, "but this being my last reply to them, I don't mind telling you that there are two, and that they are man and wife—Carl and Lya. The lady is a bit of a mystery, but if you ask my opinion I would say that she is of Mexican blood, that she was at some time or other a charmer of snakes, and that of the two she is, on the whole, the worse, although that is saying a good deal. However, all this is pure guess-work on my part, although, having seen her, I can tell you that she's a handsome piece, still a year or two on the right side of forty. And now," he said firmly, "I will speak no more of the Circus Brandt."

And we talked instead of Sarrasani, of Krone, of Carmo, and of Hagebeck.

A year passed, and I forgot the Circus Brandt, which no doubt during this period of time wandered from Tokio to San Francisco and Belgrade up to Stockholm and back again, as though the devil himself were at its heels.

And then I met an old friend, a famous juggler, whom I had not seen for many months. I offered him a drink and asked him where he had been since our last meeting. He laughed, and said that he had been in hell. I told him I was not much of a hand at riddles. He laughed again.

"Oh—hell?" he said. "Perhaps that's an exaggeration; but, anyhow, I've been as near to it as ever I want to. I've been touring with the Circus Brandt."

"The Circus Brandt?"

"Exactly. The Balkan States, Spain, North Africa. Then Holland and Belgium, and finally France. I cleared out in France. If they'd doubled my salary I'd not have stayed with them."

"Is the Circus Brandt, then," I asked, "as rough as all that?"

"Rough?" he said. "No, it's not rough. I can stick roughness. What I can't stand, however, is working with people who give me the creeps. Now you're laughing, and I'm not surprised, but I can assure you that I've lain awake at night in my wagon sweating with fear and I'm by no means a fanciful chap."

By this time I was keenly interested.

"Please tell me," I asked, "what it was that frightened you so much."

"That I can't do," he replied, and ordered another drink, "for the fact is that I, personally, was not treated badly during the tour. The Brandts were very civil to me—too civil, in fact, for they'd ask me into their wagon sometimes for a chat between shows, and I hated going—it gave me goose-flesh down my back. Somehow—and you'll laugh again I know—it was like sitting there talking to two big cats that were just waiting to pounce after they'd finished playing with you. I swear I believed, at the time, that Carl and Lya could see in the dark. Now, of course, that's ridiculous, and I know it, but I still get the creeps when I think about them. I must have been nervy—over-tired, you know, at the time."

I asked whether anyone else at the circus had been similarly affected by the Brandts, and he wrinkled his brows, as though trying to remember, with obvious distaste, any further details of his tour.

"There's one thing that happened so that all could see," he remarked after a pause, "and that was in a wild part of Rumania, somewhere near the Carpathian mountains. We were passing through a little village, on our way to a town a few miles' distance, and the peasants came flocking out to

5

watch us pass, which was, of course, only natural, for the show is a very fine one. Then, in the village street, a van stuck, and the Brandts came out of their big living-wagon to see what had happened."

"Well?" I asked, for he paused again.

"Well, it was funny, that's all. They scattered like rabbits—rushed into their cottages and banged the doors. The wagon was shoved out of the rut and we went on, but in the next village there was no sign of life, for everything was deserted and the doors were barred. But on every door was nailed a wreath of garlic flowers."

"Anything else?" I asked, for he had relapsed into silence.

"Oh, one little thing I remember noticing. The menagerie. The Brandts seldom bother to inspect that part of the show. They're too busy about the ring and the ticket office. But one day she—Mme Brandt—had to go through the horse-tent and the menagerie to find some agent who was talking to the boys there. It really was a bit odd—the noise was blood-curdling. It was as though the lions and tigers were frightened; not angry, you know, or roaring for their food, but quite a different sort of row. And, when she had gone, the horses were sweating. I felt 'em myself, and it was a chilly day."

"Really," I said, "it's time you came back."

"Oh," he replied. "I don't expect you to believe me. Why should you? I wouldn't have talked if you hadn't asked me about the Circus Brandt. I'd just have said I was glad to be home. But as you asked me ... Oh, well, one day I'll tell you why I left them in France. It's not a pretty story. But I won't tell it tonight. I avoid the Brandts as a bedtime topic—I've been dreaming about them lately."

It took me some time to coax the juggler's tale from him. One morning, however, as we were walking along the Unter den Linden, in pale but radiant spring sunshine, he consented to tell it. Translated into English, this is the story:

While the Circus Brandt was touring Northern Africa, when it was, in fact, only a few days from Tangier, a man arrived asking for work. He was, he said, an Alsatian, and had been a stoker, but his ship had abandoned him at Tangier, and he had been seeking a job ever since. This man was interviewed by Carl Brandt himself, who had been accosted by him on the lot. They were a curiously contrasted pair as they stood talking together outside the steps of the Brandt's palatial living-wagon. The Alsatian was fair, a big handsome young man with thick, blond haîr, a tanned skin and honest, rather stupid, blue eyes. Carl Brandt was tall, too, but emaciated, wasted, and swarthy dark; he had a smooth, darting black head like a snake's head; his long face was haggard, and yellow as old ivory; he wore a tiny dark imperial beard; his black eyes were feverishly alive in heavy purple hollows, and his teeth were sharp and broken and rotten. He was said to take drugs, and indeed he had very much the appearance of an addict. While the two men were talking the door of the wagon opened and Mme Brandt appeared on the threshold, asking her husband what the stranger wanted of him. She herself was, incidentally, a remarkably handsome woman, although no longer young. She was powerfully but gracefully made, with quantities of shining blue-black hair, delicate features, oblique, heavy-lidded eyes, and one of those opaque white skins that always look like milk. She had no colour, but was all black and white. Even her lips were pale, not being painted, and her face was heart-shaped against the shadow of her dark hair. She wore white in hot countries and black in the north, but somehow one never noticed that she was not dressed in colours. She seldom looked at the person to whom she was talking, so that when she did it was rather a shock. Her voice was low, and she never showed her teeth, making one imagine that they must be bad, like her husband's.

Both Brandts stayed talking to the Alsatian for about ten minutes in the hot sunshine. It was impossible to eavesdrop, but once the Alsatian was heard reiterating rather warmly that he was a stoker by profession. Finally, however, Carl Brandt took the man off to the head keeper of the menagerie and said that he was to be given work. The Alsatian for his part said that his name was Anatole, and that he was used to rough jobs. Soon afterwards the circus went on towards Tunis.

The new hand, Anatole, was a good-natured, genial, simple fellow, who soon became popular, not only with the tent-men and grooms, but also with the more democratic of the performers, who amused themselves, during the tedium of long "jumps", by making him sing to them, for he had a rich and beautiful voice. Generally he sang German *Lieder* or long-forgotten French music-hall songs, but sometimes he favoured them with snatches of roaring, racy, impudent bal-lads couched in an *argot* with which they were every one unfamiliar. On one occasion, before the evening show, when Anatole was shouting one of these coarsely cheerful songs inside the Big Top, the flap was suddenly opened to reveal Mme Brandt's pale, watchful face in the aperture.

Instantly, although some of the small audience had not seen her, a curious discomfort fell upon the gay party. Ana-tole, whose back was turned towards the entrance, immedi-ately became aware of some strain or tension among his listeners, and, wheeling round, stopped abruptly in the middle of a bar. The little group scrambled awkardly to its feet.

Mme Brandt murmured in her low voice:

"Don't let me interfere with your concert, my friends. Go on, you"—to Anatole—"that's a lively song you were singing. Where did you pick it up?"

Anatole, standing respectfully before her, was silent. Mme Brandt did not look at him or seem to concern herself with him in any way, but sent her oblique eyes roving over the empty seats of the great tent, yet somehow, in some curious way, it became obvious to her listeners that she was stubbornly determined to drag from him an answer.

Anatole at length muttered :

"I learned the song, madame, on board a Portuguese fruit-trader many years ago."

Mme Brandt made no sign of having heard him speak.

After this incident, however, she began to employ the odd hand on various jobs about her own living-wagon, with the result that he had less time to sing and not much time even for his work in the menagerie. Anatole, good-humoured and jovial as he was, soon conceived a violent dislike of the proprietress, and he took no pains to hide it from his friends, who were incidentally in hearty agreement with him on this point. Everyone hated the Brandts; many feared them.

The circus crossed to Spain and began to tour Andalusia. Several performers left; new acts were promptly engaged. Carl Brandt had always found it easy to rid himself of artists. Ten minutes before the show was due to open he would send for some unlucky trapezist and, pointing to the man's apparatus, complicated and heavy, slung up to one of the big poles, he would say casually :

"I want you to move that to the other side of the tent before the show."

The artist would perhaps laugh, thinking the director was making some obscure joke.

Brandt would then continue, gently :

"You had better hurry, don't you think?"

The artist would protest indignantly.

"It's impossible, sir. How can I move my apparatus in ten minutes?"

Brandt would then watch him, sneering, for a few seconds. Then he would turn away, saying suavely :

"Discharged for insubordination," and walk off to telegraph to his agent for a new act.

Mme Brandt took a curious pleasure in teasing Anatole.

46

She knew that he feared her, and it amused her to send for him, to keep him standing in her wagon while she polished her nails or sewed or wrote letters, utterly indifferent to his presence. After about ten minutes she would look up, glancing at some point above his head, and ask him, in her soft, languid voice, if he liked circus life, and whether he was happy with them. She would chat for some time, casually asking him searching questions about the other performers, then suddenly she would look direct at him, with a strange, brooding stare, while she said:

"Better than tramp ships, isn't it, eh? You are more comfortable here than you were as a stoker, I suppose?"

Sometimes she would add:

"Tell me something about a stoker's life, Anatole. What were your duties, and your hours?"

Always, when she dismissed him, his hair was damp with sweat.

The Circus Brandt wandered gradually northwards towards the Basque country, until the French border was almost in sight. They were to cut across France into Belgium and Holland, then back again. The Brandts could never stay long anywhere. Just before the circus entered French territory Anatole gave his notice to the head keeper. He was a hard worker and so popular with his mates that the keeper went grumbling to Carl Brandt, who agreed to an increase of salary. Anatole refused to stay on.

Mme Brandt was in the wagon when this news was told to her husband. She said to Carl: "If you want the Alsatian to stay, I will arrange it. Leave it to me. I think I understand the trouble, and, as you say, he is a useful man."

The next day she sent for Anatole, and after ignoring him for about five minutes she asked him listlessly what he meant by leaving them. Anatole, standing rigid near the door, stammered some awkward apology.

"Why is it?"

"I have—I have had offered me a job."

"Better than this?" she pursued, stitching at her work.

"Yes, madame."

"Yet," she continued idly, "you were happy with us in Africa, happy in Spain. Why not, then, in France?"

"Madame—"

She snapped a thread with her teeth.

"Why not in France, Anatole?"

There was no reply.

Suddenly she flung her sewing to the ground and fixed him with an unswerving glance. Something leaped into her eyes that startled him, an ugly, naked, hungry look that he had never before seen there. Her eyes burned him, like a devil's eyes. She said, speaking rapidly, scarcely moving her lips:

"I will tell you why you are afraid of France, shall I, Anatole? I have guessed your secret, my friend. . . . You are a deserter from the Foreign Legion, and you are afraid of being recaptured. This is it, isn't it? Oh, don't trouble to lie; I have known ever since we were in Africa. It's true, isn't it, what I have said?"

He shook his head, swallowing, unable to speak.

It was a hot day and he wore only a thin shirt. In a second she sprang from her chair across the wagon and threw herself upon him, tearing at this garment with her fingers. Terrified, he struggled, but she was too swift, too violent, too relentless. The shirt ripped in two and revealed upon his white chest the seam of livid scars.

"Bullet wounds!" she laughed in his ear. "A stoker with bullet wounds! I was right, wasn't I, Anatole?"

He was conscious, above his fear, of a strange shrinking sensation of repulsion at her proximity. "God," he thought, "she's after me!" And he was sickened, as some people are sickened by the sight of a deadly snake. And then, surprisingly, he was saved. She darted away from him, sank down in her chair, snatched up her sewing.

Her quick ear had heard the footsteps of Carl Brandt.

Anatole stood there dazed, clutching the great rent in his shirt. Carl Brandt entered the wagon softly, for he always wore rubber soles to his shoes. His wife addressed him in her low unflurried voice.

"You see Anatole there? He has just been telling me why he is afraid to come with us to France. He is a deserter from the Foreign Legion. Look at the wounds there, on his chest."

Anatole gazed helplessly at the long, yellow face of Brandt, who stared at him for some moments in silence.

"A deserter?" Brandt said at length, and chuckled. "A deserter? You needn't be afraid, my lad, to come with us to France. They've something better to do than hunt for obscure escaped legionaries there. Oh, yes, you'll be safe enough. I'll protect you."

And he stood rubbing his hands and staring thoughtfully at Anatole with his gleaming black eyes. Anatole, to escape from them, promised to stay. He had the unpleasant sensation of having faced in the wagon that afternoon not one snake, but two. He disliked reptiles. He meant to bolt, but he had lied to Madame Brandt when he talked of a new job, and he was comfortable where he was. He was, too, an unimaginative creature, and the horrors of the Legion now seemed very remote. Soon he was in France, utterly unable to believe that he was in any danger. To his delight, his mistress ignored him after the scene in the wagon. She had obviously realised, he thought to himself, that he found her disgusting. And he would have been completely happy had he not known that he had made a dangerous enemy.

The Circus Brandt employed as lion-tamer an ex-matador, a man named "Captain" da Silva. This individual was not very pleased with his situation. He had lost his nerve about a year before, but after working the same group of lions for ten months he had become more confident and consequently more content. Then, without any warning, Carl Brandt bought a mixed group of animals, and told da Silva to start work at once. The tamer was furious. Lions, tigers, bears, and leopards! He shrugged his shoulders and obeyed sulkily. Soon the mixed group was ready for the ring, and appeared for a week with great success.

Then one morning da Silva went to the cages and found his animals in a wild, abnormal state. Snarling, bristling, foaming at the mouth, they seemed unable even to recognise their tamer. A comrade, coming to watch, whispered in his ear:

"She walked last night."

Da Silva shuddered. There was a legend in the Circus Brandt that whenever the animals were nervous or upset Lya Brandt, the "she-devil", had walked in her sleep the night before, wandering into the menagerie and terrifying the beasts, who presumably knew her for what she was.

The tiger roared, and was answered by the lioness. Da Silva turned to his companion.

"I'm off. I wouldn't work these cats tonight for a fortune."

In twenty minutes' time he was at the railway station.

Carl Brandt heard the news in silence. Then he raised his arm and struck his head keeper savagely on the mouth. Wrapping his black cloak about his tall, thin figure, he left the office and sought his own wagon. His wife was engaged drinking a cup of coffee. They eyed each other in silence.

Then she said calmly:

"It's da Silva, I suppose?"

"Da Silva, yes. Already he has gone. Now who will work the mixed group?"

She drained her cup and answered thoughtfully:

"I know of several tamers."

"Probably. And how long will they take to get here?"

"Exactly," she said pouring out more coffee. "That, I agree, is the great objection. Is there no one on the lot who could work the cats for a week or two?"

"What nonsense are you talking?"

She put her hand over her eyes.

"You seem to forget Anatole. An escaped Legionary in French territory. Would he disobey your orders, do you think?"

There was a pause.

"I'll send for him," said Brandt at length.

They were silent as they waited for the Alsatian. When he came in Lya did not look at him, but began to polish her nails.

Carl Brandt turned his yellow, wrinkled face towards Anatole. His eyes were dark and smouldering hollows. He said gently:

"You know that da Silva has left?"

"Yes, sir." Anatole was perplexed.

"There is no one now to work the animals until a new tamer is engaged."

"No, sir."

"It is not my custom to fail my patrons. I show always what I advertise. The new tamer should be here in a week. It is about this week that I wish to speak."

Another pause. Anatole's heart began to pump against his ribs.

Brandt said placidly:

"I am about to promote you, my friend. For a week you shall work the mixed group."

Anatole turned dusky red. He was furiously angry, so angry indeed that his fear of the silent woman sitting at the table vanished entirely. No longer conscious of her presence he blurted out violently:

"What! You wish me to go in the cage with those animals? Then you must find someone else; I wouldn't do it for a fortune."

Brandt smiled, showing his black, broken teeth. His wife, utterly indifferent, continued to paint her nails bright red. Brandt said pleasantly:

"Are you perhaps in a position to dictate, my friend? I may be wrong, of course, but I am under the impression that we are now in *French territory*. Charming words, eh?"

Anatole was silent. He thought suddenly and with horror of the Legion—blistering sun, filth, and brutality. He thought, too, of the salt-mines, that ghastly living death to which he would inevitably be condemned in the event of capture. Then he remembered the animals as he had last seen them, ferocious, maddened. He shook his head.

"That's bluff," he said shakily. "I'm no tamer. You can't force me into the cage."

Carl Brandt chuckled. The delicate yellow ivory of his skin seamed itself into a thousand wrinkles. He pulled out his watch.

"Five minutes, Anatole, to come with me to the menagerie. Otherwise I telephone the police. If I may be permitted to advise you, I suggest the menagerie. Even the belly of a lion is preferable, I should imagine, to the African salt-mines. But take your choice."

Madame Brandt, snapping an orange-stick in two, now obtruded herself quietly into the conversation.

"No, Anatole," she said musingly, "it will not be possible to run away in the night. The Herr Director will take trouble, great trouble, to have you traced. The Herr Director has no wish to protect criminals."

Once again she looked directly at him, fixing him with the burning and threatening glance that was like a sword.

Brandt glanced at his watch.

"I must remind you, Anatole, that you have only two minutes left," he said with an air of great courtesy. "How many years did you serve in the Legion, I wonder? And is it eight years in the salt mines for deserters, or perhaps more?"

"I'll work the animals," said Anatole shortly. He knew that Lya Brandt had read his thoughts, and wiped the sweat from his face as he went towards the menagerie. It was not possible for the mixed group to appear at the matinée, but it was announced to the circus in general that the cats would work that night without fail. Anatole was to spend the afternoon rehearsing them.

His face was grey as he shut himself in the cage, armed only with a tamer's switch. Outside the bars stood two, keepers with loaded revolvers. They, too, were nervous. The animals stood motionless to stare at the stranger, hackles raised, restless yellow eyes fixed upon him. Around the cage were arranged painted wooden pedestals, upon which the animals were trained to sit at the word of command. The Alsatian now gave that command. They took no notice. He repeated it louder, slapping the bars with his switch, and they scattered in a sudden panic to take up their accustomed seats. He pulled out the paper hoop through which the lions must jump. They snarled for several minutes, striking out with their savage paws, then, in the end, possibly deciding that obedience was less trouble, they bounded through the loop with an ill grace. The two keepers, and Anatole as well, were soon streaming with perspiration as though they had been plunged into water. The Alsatian was now, however, more confident. He turned to the bears.

Twenty minutes later Carl Brandt rejoined his wife in the living-wagon.

"Better than I expected," said the director coolly. Mme Brandt made no reply, nor did she turn her head.

That evening the Alsatian was supplied with a splendid sky-blue uniform and cherry-coloured breeches from the circus wardrobe. Out on the lot his comrades glanced at him sympathetically. One or two, unconscious of his antecedents, warned him to defy Brandt and keep out of the cage. Anatole merely shook his head, incapable of giving an explanation.

It was dusk. The bandsmen, splendid in their green and gold uniforms, played the overture inside the huge tent. A group of clowns, glittering in brilliant spangles, stood waiting to make their comic entry. Behind the clowns six or seven grooms were busy controlling twenty milk-white Arab stallions with fleecy white manes and tails. These horses were magnificent in scarlet trappings. The Chinese troupe, dark kimonos over gorgeous brocade robes, diligently practised near the bears' cage. Anatole sat on a bale of hay near the tigers, deaf to the advice muttered in his ear by various comrades. The circus proceeded.

Up in the dome of the tent two muscular young men in peach-coloured tights flung themselves from bar to bar with thrilling grace and swiftness. Down below, the attendants rapidly constructed a vast cage, staggering beneath sections of heavy iron bars. Soon the band crashed out a chord, and Anatole, the Legionary, stepped into the cage, bowing modestly in response to the applause. Then an iron door was slid aside and down the narrow tunnel crept a file of tawny shapes.

Lions, tigers, leopards, bears. Gracefully they padded into the arena, stretching themselves, rubbing against the bars of the cage, yawning at the bright lights, showing their teeth, slinking with a cat-like agility about the ring.

Gripping his switch, Anatole uttered the first command. One minute later the animals were seated with a certain docility upon their wooden pedestals. Anatole produced his hoop. At first the people of the circus held their breath, then, gradually, as five minutes passed, they relaxed. He was doing well. They sighed with relief. The climax of the act was a tableau during the course of which the animals grouped themselves, standing erect on their hind legs about the trainer, who himself sprang upon a pedestal, arm upraised to give more effect to this subjugation of the beasts. The biggest tiger lay at his feet during the tableau, and while the other animals soon assumed their accustomed positions when ordered, the tiger was at first always unwilling to fling himself upon the sawdust.

Posing the lions and leopards, Anatole, one foot on the pedestal, spoke briskly, curtly, to the great beast, which stared at him sulkily. A second passed, seeming longer than a minute to the circus watchers. The tiger continued to stare, and

Anatole, banging at the bars with his switch, pointed stubbornly at the ground at his feet.

His back was towards the ring entrance, and he did not see the grooms and attendants draw back respectfully to allow someone to pass through the red velvet curtains. His comrades did, and nudged one another, for Mme Brandt seldom came near the arena during a performance. She stood for a moment near the curtains tall and straight in her flowing white dress, her face pale against the dense blackness of her hair.

Then, suddenly, there was tumult in the peaceful cage, as snarling furiously, the animals leaped from their pedestals to dash themselves savagely against the bars. Caught by surprise, Anatole turned, slashing with his switch, shouting, oblivious of the sullen tiger behind him. A leopard, maddened with fright, collided against him and sent him stumbling to the ground. With the fierce swiftness of a mighty hawk, the great tiger sprang. A thick choking growl that made the blood run cold, yells of terror from the crowd, and then the crack of two revolver shots. Armed with hosepipes, the menagerie men drove the animals back. The tiger was wounded in the shoulder, and clawed the ground, biting at itself in a frenzy of pain.

Anatole lay doubled up on the sawdust looking like a rag dummy, so limp and twisted was his body. On the bright blue of his uniform oozed a clotted stream of red. His face? Anatole had no longer a face; only a huge and raw and gaping wound. Opening a side door, they dragged his body from the cage and swiftly wrapped it in the gorgeous coat of a Chinese acrobat standing near by. Screaming, weeping, cursing, the horrified audience fought, struggled and stampeded to leave the tent. In the noise and tumult, Mme Brandt slipped through the red velvet curtains and vanished like a white shadow.

That night the body was laid temporarily in a little canvas

dressing-room belonging to the clowns. It was late before the show people retired to bed, but by one o'clock in the morning all was still in the tent-town of Brandt's Circus. Only the night watchman, a stolid, unimaginative fellow, paced slowly up and down, swinging his lantern, but from time to time a lion would whimper and growl in the silence of the night.

It was the watchman, however, who afterwards related to his comrades what he saw during this lonely vigil ... It was about an hour before dawn, and the man was lolling on a heap of hay, relieved, no doubt, to think the night would soon be over, when all at once his quick ear caught the soft sound of approaching footsteps. He turned, hiding his lantern beneath his coat. It was Mme Brandt, of course, walking slowly, like a sleep-walker, across the deserted arena towards the dressing-rooms, seeming no more tangible than a shadow, a white shadow that gleamed for a moment in the darkness, and then was gone, swallowed by the gloom of the night. Now, the watchman was a brave fellow, and inclined to be inquisitive. He slipped off his shoes and crept after her.

Madame Brandt glided straight to the little dressing-room wherein lay the mangled body of the Legionary. The watchman had not dared to bring his lantern, and it was, therefore, difficult for him to see what was happening, but at the same time he managed to observe quite enough. He glimpsed her white figure kneeling near the dark shape on the floor; as he watched, she struggled with some drapery or other, and he saw that she was trying to drag away the sheet that covered the corpse. Having apparently achieved her purpose, she remained still for a moment, staring at what she saw; this immobility, which lasted only for a second, was succeeded by a sudden revulsion of feeling more horrible than anything that had gone before; for with all the ferocity of a starving animal she flung herself upon the body, shaking it, gripping it tightly to steady its leaden weight while she thrust her face, her mouth, down upon that torn and bleeding throat ... then in the distant menagerie the lions and tigers broke the silence of the night with sudden tumult.

"Yes," said the juggler, after a pause, "we liked Anatole. He was a good comrade, although, mind you, he had probably been a murderer, and most certainly a thief. But in the Circus Brandt, you know, that means nothing at all."

"Where is the Circus Brandt now?" I asked, after another pause.

He shrugged his shoulders.

"Poland, I think, or possibly Peru. How can I tell? The Brandts are gipsies, nomads, here today, gone tomorrow. Possibly they travel fast because there is always something to hush up. But who can say? The devil has an admirable habit of looking after his friends."

I was silent, for I was thinking both of Lya Brandt and Anatole. Suddenly I felt rather sick.

www.ingramcontent.com/pod-product-compliance
Lightning Source LLC
Chambersburg PA
CBHW020733250626
47155CB00006B/2275